THE RABBIT
John Burningham

GW00390808

Jonathan Cape Thirty Bedford Square London

We have a rabbit

The rabbit has a hutch in the garden

His favourite food
is dandelions

I like to stroke
the rabbit

Sometimes the rabbit
gets out

He likes to hop about
in the garden

I would like him to stay
in the garden, but
he eats Daddy's plants

So I have to catch him

And put him back

**Other Little Books
by John Burningham**

THE BABY

THE SCHOOL

THE SNOW